Motherlove

By Virginia Kroll

Illustrated by Lucia Washburn

Dawn Publications

For Helen Kroll, my mother, and for Aunts Stephanna Niziol, Babs Halvorsen, and Jeanette Cicatello, Godmother Karen Murphy, Grandma Grace Meyers and friend Heather Brechtel—the others who nurture my children and me. —VK

To Megan. —LW

Library of Congress Cataloging-in-Publication Data

Kroll, Virginia L.
    Motherlove / by Virginia Kroll ; illustrated by
Lucia Washburn. – 1st ed.
        p. cm.
    SUMMARY: A look at a variety of species,
including our own, in which mothers nurture their
young.
    ISBN: 1-883220-81-5 (case)
    ISBN: 1-883220-80-7 (pbk.)

    1. Parental behavior in animals—Juvenile
literature. 2. Mothers—Juvenile literature. I.
Washburn, Lucia, ill. II Title.

QL 751.5.K76 1998   591.56'3
                              QBI98-691

Dawn Publications
14618 Tyler Foote Road
Nevada City, CA 95959
800-545-7475
Email: DawnPub@oro.net
Website: www.DawnPub.com

Printed in China on recycled paper

10 9 8 7 6 5 4 3 2 1
First Edition

Cover design by Renee Glenn Designs
Computer production by Rob Froelick

0116610 0

Some mothers are furry.

Llamas have long fur to keep them warm in a high mountain climate. Like all mammals, they feed milk to their young, and are warm-blooded, which means that their bodies maintain a constant temperature regardless of how hot or cold it is outside.

Some mothers are purry;
all mothers are wonderfully warm.

*Purring is a vibrating sound of contentment made in
the throats of many cats, both wild and domestic.*

They cradle and cuddle
and coddle and huddle
and spread out their wings in a storm.

Like many birds, these mute swans sit carefully atop their babies. When the nestlings are older, parent birds shield them with their wings from wet or chilly weather.

They scoop out a space in the coziest place, just right for their babies' upbringing,

Polar bear mothers scoop out a den to make a snow cave where they give birth and rear their cubs. Most creatures create similar snug places, and other names for them are nests, haunts, burrows, coverts, nurseries, lairs, and aeries.

Then lull them to sleep with a chortle or cheep or sweet cooing or lullaby-singing.

In spring, the father dove makes loud cooing noises to announce the dove family's territory, while the mother makes soft cooing noises in the nest. To humans, the coos sound mournful, which is why they are called "mourning doves." Many mothers, including humans, sing or make other comforting sounds to soothe their little ones.

Moms help with the preening;
they're endlessly cleaning
and giving out good things to eat.

Mother sea otters, like many animal mothers, teach their young how to preen, or groom, their fur or feathers. This helps distribute body oils and circulate air properly so that the animal stays warm and, in some cases, waterproof.

They wait for the slow while uplifting the low with support, till they're back on their feet.

Mothers move more slowly than other animals, keeping their young within sight or calling range. Some large mammals, like white-tailed deer, nudge and prod their young, encouraging them to stand strongly on their own.

They're good at respecting,
directing, protecting
and teaching their offspring to fly.

They separate hagglers
and bring in the stragglers
and know when (or not) to ask why.

Young creatures have strong instincts, a powerful inborn drive that naturally leads them to do things a certain way. Even so, the parents of some animals, such as barn owls, must also teach their babies some things, such as how to fly and hunt for food.

Animals have signals to alert others of their kind to danger.
Meerkat colonies, for example, protect their young and one another
by posting a sentinel, or "watch meerkat," to warn of intruders.

They ward off the strangers
and warn of the dangers
by hinting with signals and cues.

They soothe their youngs' pain;
help them weather the rain,
then find rainbows to banish the blues.

Orangutans and some other large primates use giant leaves as umbrellas. Many animals protect their young physically from storms. Human mothers do what they can to ease their children's emotional pain, as well.

Some mothers are called 'mama,' 'mommy,' or 'mam.'

In many languages, the word for "mother" resembles the first sounds babies make. Other names include mum, mummy, mammy, ma and marmie (English), mére (French), madré (Spanish), Mutter (German), moeder (Dutch), matka (Polish), máthair (Irish), ema (Mbuti), and ima (Arabic).

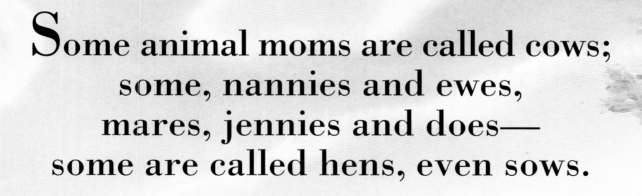

Some animal moms are called cows;
some, nannies and ewes,
mares, jennies and does—
some are called hens, even sows.

"Cow" is the name given to a mature female elephant, rhinoceros, walrus, whale, seal or bovine animal. Besides being a child's caretaker, a nanny is a female goat. Ewes are female sheep. Mares are female horses, zebras, or donkeys, although female donkeys are also called jennies. Does are female deer, rabbits, hares, ferrets, rats and kangaroos. Hens are female fowl. A sow is a female pig, bear, badger, guinea pig or hedgehog.

Some moms have one baby and others have two. Some mommies have three —even more!

The number of young, or offspring, varies vastly among species. Humans, marine mammals and some large mammals such as these Dall sheep most often have one at a time. Bears, large cats and large birds such as these golden eagles have two or three. Many rodents such as ground squirrels have between two and eight. Opossums can have ten or more. Some fishes and reptiles can bear 50 or more live young at one time. Egg laying animals can have thousands.

They rest in tall trees,
under rocks, in the seas,
on cliffsides or sands by the shore.

Wherever there is a suitable place, some creature will nest. California sea lions relax on rocky shores while cormorants lay eggs higher up on bare, rocky cliff ledges. Some birds even lay eggs on the ground.

Some "moms" needn't even
be mothers at all,
but grannies or friends, even aunties.

But however they're known,
they put heart into homes
whether houses or castles or shanties.

Certain species, like bats, wolves, whales, and humans, of course, will adopt orphaned or needy young as their own. Foster mothers and adoptive mothers can be as loving and caring as biological mothers.

Some mothers must heave
when their offspring should leave;
they're terrific at pushing and shoving.

In order to give birth, mammal mothers must labor, or work at pushing their babies out into the world. A mother gray whale receives help from another female who assists with the birth and then helps hoist the newborn up to the surface so it can take its first breath.

But whoever they are and whatever they're called, they all are fantastic at loving!

Mothers spend their lives training their young to go out on their own. But even when they are gone from their nests or homes, they remain in their mothers' hearts forever.

ALTHOUGH **VIRGINIA KROLL** IS A WELL-PUBLISHED AUTHOR, she is a mother first and foremost. She is married to David Haeick and has three sons, three daughters, and a granddaughter, all living either at home or close by her near Buffalo, New York. Her mothering extends also to her "family" of pets, which currently includes two dogs, nine cats, five rabbits, two fish, eight birds, two turtles, two gerbils and twelve guinea pigs. She expresses her love and concern for all of Earth's peoples in another book published by Dawn Publications, *With Love, to Earth's Endangered Peoples.*

LUCIA WASHBURN ILLUSTRATED THIS BOOK while her two-year-old daughter, Megan, played with crayons at her own little table nearby, or looked at animal pictures in a pile of reference books. Lucia loves mothering and illustrating. She is a graduate of the Rhode Island School of Design, and lives in Petaluma, California. This is the fourth book she has illustrated, the first for Dawn Publications.

BOOKS ABOUT APPRECIATING OTHERS FROM DAWN PUBLICATIONS

With Love, to Earth's Endangered Peoples, by Virginia Kroll. All over the world, groups of people, like species of animals, are endangered. Their age-old ways of living are in danger of being lost forever. Often these people have a beautiful, meaningful relationship with the Earth, and with each other. This book portrays several of them, with love.

Walking with Mama, by Barbara White Stynes. What sweet intimacy a mother and child share when walking together in nature! Mother and child not only discover the wonders of nature but also deepen the wonders of love.

Stickeen: John Muir and the Brave Little Dog, by John Muir as retold by Donnell Rubay. Surrounded by deep canyons of ice, John Muir and a little black dog wonder—are they doomed? How they handle the challenge, and are changed by it, creates a classic story—"the most memorable of all my wild days," as Muir later wrote of this 1880 adventure in Alaska.

Grandpa's Garden, by Shea Darien. On Saturdays, Grandpa and grandchild work side by side in Grandpa's garden. Among the radishes and rhubarb they share their deepest feelings and wishes. They harvest love and wisdom along with peas and turnips. First hand they learn of life and death, growth and change.

DAWN PUBLICATIONS is dedicated to inspiring in children a deeper understanding and appreciation for all life on Earth. To order, or for a free copy of our catalog, please call 800-545-7475. Please also visit our web site at www.DawnPub.com.